Pauline Carrington Rust

Legend of the Luray Caverns

founded upon the discovery of a skelton in one of its chasms

Pauline Carrington Rust

Legend of the Luray Caverns
founded upon the discovery of a skelton in one of its chasms

ISBN/EAN: 9783337391355

Printed in Europe, USA, Canada, Australia, Japan

Cover: Foto ©Andreas Hilbeck / pixelio.de

More available books at **www.hansebooks.com**

LEGENDS OF THE LURAY CAVERNS.

Founded Upon the discovery of a Skeleton in one of its chasms

BY PAULINE CARRINGTON RUST.

Published and Designed BY LOUGHEAD & Co.

1110 WALNUT

PHILADELPHIA.

1302 Gilbert St.
Feb. 22, 1887.

Dear Mr. Corson,

In my visit to Luray Cave, in
the summer of 1880, I had the opportunity
of seeing and satisfying myself of
the authenticity of the human
bones, found embedded in the
rocky floor of the cave. The
bones of the _bear_, which infests
caves, _bear_ so near a resemblance
to human bones that they are
often mistaken for such when
found under similar circum-

stances. Then however I recognized as the femur and tibia of an adult man, partially embedded and partially protruding from the rock. In our recent visit together, I found the same bones much mutilated and scarcely recognizable. At your request I broke off a fragment of the femur for examination. It is chalky and friable and strongly adherent to a portion of the rocky crust. I observe that its condition of preservation is identical

with that of bones of the extinct peccary and other associated animals found under similar circumstances in other cave deposits of Virginia, and this has led me to conjecture that the man of Luray is more ancient than has been supposed, and probably belonged to a prehistoric race.

Sincerely yours,
Joseph Leidy.

·THE LEGEND·

Long, bright shafts of yellow sunshine
Cleft the mountain's purple height,
Spanned in lines of broken glory
All Gerando's * rushing might.

Shot in quivering golden arrows
Through the sombre, sighing pines,
And were lost amid the forest,
In the shadows' deepening lines.

*Original name of the Shenandoah River.

1

ALL was still that summer morning;
  Silence seemed to pause and grow,
Till the forest hushed to listen
  To the river singing low.

Through the dark depths of the forest,
  Following close the tortuous path,
Came a band of stern faced warriors
  To appease their chieftain's wrath.

2

KILL BUCK, chief of the Catawbas,
Had an oath of vengeance sworn
'Gainst the young brave Messinetto,*
Who had dared the nation's scorn.

SILENTLY they came as shadows,
Till they reached the river's main,
While no sound broke on the stillness
Save Gerando's low refrain.

*Messinetto, the original name of Massanutton.

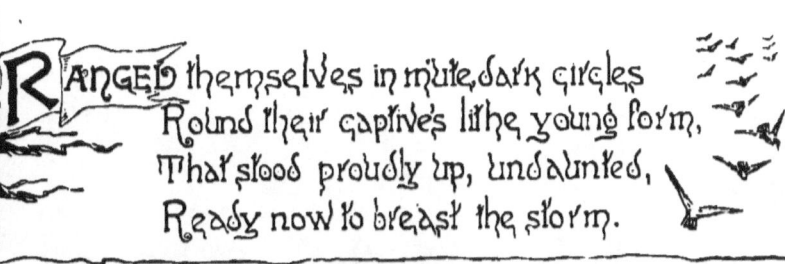

RANGED themselves in mute, dark circles
　　Round their captive's lithe young form,
　　That stood proudly up, undaunted,
　　Ready now to breast the storm.

THEN uprose their haughty Chieftain,
　　And the heavy silence broke;
　　Did no thrill of pity stir them,
　　As they heard the words he spoke.

4

"Ye have come this day my brothers—
Twenty warriors bold and strong,
Ye shall hear the shameful story,
And avenge Wahnona's wrong.

Manito, the Mighty, hear us!
Hear the solemn vow now sworn!
Though no Chieftain's blood shall stain us,
Death for falsehood shall be borne!

Thou wert false, Oh Messinetto,
  False to squaw, and sire, and race,
And thy blood, Oh Messinetto,
  Cannot wash out thy disgrace!

Thou hast left thy red faced brothers,
  Mated with the pale-face dove,
Bear our curse, Oh Messinetto,
  Endless death for faithless love!

6

"Thou shalt perish, Messinetto,
    Far away from name and race,
  Where the smile of the Great Spirit
    Will not touch thy burial place!

And no dream shall cross thy vision;
    In the slumber thou shalt keep,
  Shut from sound, and light, and motion,
    In the Earth's breast fathoms deep.

7

Neath yon hill there lies a cavern—
  In its depths shall be thy grave;
  All its splendors are befitting
  Burial place of Indian Brave;

All its walls are strangely sculptured—
  Column high and chasm wide;
  'Tis the place where all the shadows
  Of the past years, silent hide.

"Ye have heard me now, my brothers—
Messinetto's race is run;
And the oath we swear this morning
Shall be kept ere set of sun."

Then a gasping sigh of horror
Through the tree tops made them shiver,
And there crept a sound of wailing
In the low song of the river.

9

* * * * * * * * * * * * * * * * * * *

（

()

ERE the moon rose o'er the mountain,
Hidden deep from human eye,
They had left their mute young victim
There; to slowly starve and die.

BUT that lone grave is discovered;
And to-day the hurrying tread
Of an eager throng breaks rudely
On the silence of the dead.

10

In the vast and solemn grandeur
Of the wondrous Luray cave,
Messinetto's bones are lying
In a strange and stately grave.

This is what the river told me,
As I listened to it's song —
Caught the burden of it's sorrow,
Spelled its tale of love and wrong.

FINIS

www.ingramcontent.com/pod-product-compliance
Lightning Source LLC
Chambersburg PA
CBHW030916260626
47169CB00008B/2876